BROWN   OCTOBER 2019

Ac

ACADIE

DAVE HUTCHINSON

A TOM DOHERTY ASSOCIATES BOOK

NEW YORK

This is a work of fiction. All of the characters, organizations, and events portrayed in this novella are either products of the author's imagination or are used fictitiously.

ACADIE

Copyright © 2017 by Dave Hutchinson

Cover art by Stephen Youll
Cover design by Christine Foltzer

Edited by Lee Harris

A Tor.com Book
Published by Tom Doherty Associates
175 Fifth Avenue
New York, NY 10010

www.tor.com

Tor® is a registered trademark of
Macmillan Publishing Group, LLC.

ISBN 978-0-7653-9825-3 (ebook)
ISBN 978-0-7653-9826-0 (trade paperback)

First Edition: September 2017

Acadie

IT WAS THE MORNING after the morning after my hundred and fiftieth birthday, and a terrible noise was trying to wake me up.

I stayed asleep while my subconscious did all the work and sorted through the menu of possible noises that might have been annoying enough to disturb me. Doorbell? Disconnected it. Kitchen? Been incapable of cooking anything since the day before yesterday. Decompression alarm? Not humanly possible to do anything when you hear a decompression alarm but grab an emergency suit or head for a panic room. Phone? Turned it off and only one person had the codes to turn it back on.

Ah, bollocks.

"*What?*" I muttered.

"Well, good *morning*, Mr. President," a voice purred just in front of my face. "And how *are* we today?"

"Not funny," I said. "Not funny at all."

"We've got a situation," she said.

"*You've* got a situation," I told her. "I'm still on leave."

"Sorry, this needs command authority."

"You've *got* command authority, for Christ's sake."

"Not for this. There's been an incursion."

I groaned. "It's a rock. It's *always* a rock."

"No such luck," she said. "Get over to the office, Duke. This is the real thing." And she added brightly, "And it happened on your watch. How great is that?"

I opened my eyes and my spirit recoiled. "Where?" The voice reeled off a thirty-digit string of numbers which, even after a hundred years, was still mostly meaningless to me. "That's pretty deep downsystem, isn't it?"

"Man gets a cigar," she said.

"How did the dewline miss it?"

"This is just one of the many questions we're asking ourselves at the moment. You see? An actual situation. Come on, Duke, get your game face on. Up and at 'em." And she hung up.

I stayed in my cocoon for a few more moments, looking around the bedroom. It was a nice bedroom, roomy and dark blue and almost completely spherical, its walls covered in recessed handles for cupboards and drawers. Some of my clothes were drifting gently across my field of view. It was a really nice bedroom, but I wasn't going to get to stay in it much longer today. I crossed my eyes and concentrated, and a complex of cells, grown on the surface of my liver without my knowledge or permission during some tweak or other, began to do a magic trick on my hangover. It was a big hangover, and the magic trick was going to take a little while. It was going to need fuelling or I was going to wind up hypoglycaemic, so I split open the seams of the cocoon and drifted across the bedroom until I hit the opposite wall, where I tugged at the door handle.

The moment the door opened the cats barrelled in, squeaking and spitting and twisting in the air, the black one chasing the white one. The black one hard-landed on the far wall on all four feet, bounced off, and caught the white one in midair, and they became a furious ball of black and white fur from which screeching noises erupted.

"Stop fighting," I told them as I made my way out into the main room of the apartment. They ignored me. "Okay," I muttered. "Fine. Carry on fighting." I'd inherited the cats, along with the apartment, from an upsystem miner who had suffered a fatal but ill-defined accident. He had been, by all accounts, a colossal son of a bitch who had abused his pets. I was entirely opposed to animal cruelty, but I drew the line at sharing my bedroom with a pair of freefall cats.

I drifted into the kitchen and switched on the coffee maker, then I went into the bathroom, strapped on the breathing mask, and hung in the centre of the room while jets of very hot water beat me up. When the cycle finished, I switched it on again. Then once more for luck. Then I let the pumps drain the room and the hot-air blowers dry me off and went back into the kitchen to root around for something to eat. There wasn't much, but the coffee maker provided a large bulb of a hot caffeine-containing fluid, which was important because the complex of magic cells on the surface of my liver metabolised caffeine in order to do their thing. If they didn't have caffeine, they metabolised blood sugar, but that wasn't recommended. It was not coffee as I remembered it, though, because the Writers had still not managed to get coffee to grow in zero-gee. You'd think that would be a simple thing for smart people, particularly smart people whose previous lives had pretty much been fuelled by coffee and complex carbohydrates, but no. I drank the large bulb and refilled it and dug out some clothes that didn't smell too much, then I put a wingsuit on over them, opened the front door, and stood on the porch.

The view from my porch was pretty special, even in an age of wonders. I looked out through a scene that was like a wraparound rain forest, the mutant kudzu that half-filled the hab and gave it its structural strength as well as taking care of certain aspects of life support. It was green and misty and cool and hundreds of little specks were unhurriedly winging through it, swooping gracefully around bracing roots almost a metre thick.

A couple of the specks flapped by, Kids with great angel wings. They waved as they passed and made a couple of incomprehensible jokes and I waved back and told them to go fuck themselves, and in this way the hab became aware that its President was up and about and pretty much as grumpy as usual and all was right with the world.

Which it wasn't.

I made sure the door behind me was locked, then I flung open my arms and jumped out into the yawning green cavern of my home.

———————

I hated freefall. It had taken me at least ten years and some careful tweaking by the Writers to get over the constant nausea and terror of crashing to the ground, but I had never grown to like it. I also hated flying. The Kids made it look easy and graceful, but it was fucking hard work and I never had got the hang of it. One of my first actions as President had been to table Bills to build a monorail system in some of the larger habs and to make personal jet-packs legal in all of them, but the Council had vetoed them. I might have been President, but the Council paid no attention to me at all until something went wrong.

City Hall was near the centre of the hab, nestled in the heart of a huge clump of kudzu. I managed an untidy landing on the verandah, stripped off my wingsuit, and went inside.

Like pretty much every other building in the Colony, City Hall was a sphere of construction polyp, but it was the biggest and oldest structure here, a gnarled pearlescent ball the size of an ocean liner. It was big enough, in the event of a very, very large disaster, to act as a panic room for the whole population of the hab, but most of the time it was all but empty, occupied by skeleton staffs of administrators and engineers and techs.

It also housed my office, which was nothing much to boast about. I hadn't spent more than fifty minutes there since my term began eight months ago, and I couldn't in all honesty have directed anyone through City Hall's winding tunnels to find it.

Fortunately, I wasn't going to my office. I was going to The Office, which was easier to find because it was much bigger and located right at the heart of the structure. It was also, when I finally emerged from the tunnel, full of worried-looking people having hushed conversations over monitors and tapboards and in front of infosheets.

"Happy birthday," Connie said as I drifted over.

"Hm," I said. "So, what have we got?"

"We've got a bogey," she said, and she pointed to a big infosheet on the other side of the room. The infosheet showed a depthless field of black, and right in the middle of it floated a probe. It was about fifteen metres long and five wide, an off-white cylinder with the letters *BoC* stencilled on the side. At one end was a big fat conical meteorite shield of spun ice, and at the other was the skinny bell-shape of a high-yield fission engine exhaust. In between was a lumpy, cluttered landscape of hyperdrive motor radomes and sensor pods and squeeze-fusion microquads. It was a fairly simple design, cheap to manufacture; the Bureau of Colonisation built hundreds of them every year and sent them off on fast-flyby missions to unmapped solar systems. My heart sank.

"Not a rock, then," Connie said.

"Not a rock," I agreed. I swore. "Where's this picture coming from?"

She told me, and I swore some more. A lot more.

The Colony didn't have a government, as such. Each hab elected an annual representative to a sort of loose advisory body that kind of kept things bumping along. On the principle that anyone seeking political power wasn't to be trusted with it, the only people who were allowed on the advisory body were those who absolutely did not want to be on it. This included pretty much everyone, so the two or three months leading up to elections saw a flurry of pantomime campaigning enthusiastic enough to disqualify each candidate from office. I'd done some good campaigning myself in the past and managed to dodge the bullet, but last time the elections came round I'd been outsystem, giving someone a lift to Nova California. This had been taken as a sign that I couldn't be bothered with politics, and when I got back I found that not only had I been elected but the sneaky bastards had decided my absence proved I truly didn't give a shit and had made me President.

The office of President actually had very little real power. What it did have was a lot of responsibility, of the kind when something is such a hot potato that everyone looks around for someone else to offload it onto. That was me, for the next three and a half years or so. President of the Colony, doer of things nobody else wanted or could be bothered to do, taker of decisions so shitty nobody else wanted to be responsible for them.

If you live all your life on a planet, one of the fundamental things you never really appreciate about space is that, mostly, it all looks the same.

Obviously, there are some caveats to this. Close in to stars or orbiting planets or skirting the edge of a nebula, the scenery can be pretty spectacular. But everywhere else is just stars and emptiness.

That's pretty much all you'll see, even inside a solar system. The movies will kid you that starships zip in and out of hyperspace and pop into systems and see all the planets and asteroids and stuff, but even a solar system with dozens of planets is mostly empty space; if you're unfortunate or even just mildly inattentive it's perfectly possible to fly entirely through one and not see anything but the tiny bright point of the system's sun. At a distance of forty-five AUs, which was where we were, it's not all that hard to miss noticing the sun at all, if it's crappy enough.

At this distance, there was almost as much illumination from the stars as there was from the sun, so we had to use searchlights and image amps to see the probe. The light reflected from the thing's hull washed out the stars. It had come a long way; the conical ice shield looked pitted and eroded.

"And you shot it down," I said.

"Well, not *down*, as such," said Karl.

I ignored him and raised an eyebrow at Ernie, who just sighed and puffed out her cheeks.

"That thing's radioactive as a bastard," Karl noted. "Are we safe this close to it?"

"Cheap fucking fission drive," Ernie muttered. "Dropping it into *my* system." She was heavily modded—four arms, hands where her feet should have been, face rewritten into a gargoyle's leer that had no practical purpose, as far as I could see, aside from being off-putting.

"And you shot it down," I said again in an attempt to regain control of the situation.

"Aw, come on, Duke," she complained, gesturing with all four hands at once. "What was I supposed to do?"

"You know what you were supposed to do," I told her. "You were supposed to run silent and watch the damn thing *go away*."

"Dewline didn't pick it up," she said.

"And much brighter people than you or me are thinking about that right now," I said. "Your job was to call in the sighting and let the thing go, not fire on it."

The three of us were crammed into the control bubble of Ernie's ship, which wasn't a whole lot bigger than the probe. She spent months on her own out here in the system's halo, towing a couple of small hab modules fitted out with centrifuge equipment and smelters and chondrite refineries, mining dead comets for rare-earth metals. When she spotted the probe, she'd dropped the habs and set off in pursuit, and when she was within range she'd cooked it with a mining maser, fired a tether at it, spent almost a fortnight braking it down below solar escape velocity, and towed it back upsystem. *Then* she'd called us. Not a single one of these actions was in the standard operating procedure.

"You think it got a message out?" Karl said.

I looked at the screen in front of me, the probe floating innocently at the end of its tether.

"Let's hope not," I said. "Otherwise we're all going to be looking for somewhere else to live."

———

"No offence," said Shaker, "but for a bunch of supposedly bright people, you guys do some stupid things sometimes."

"Leaving aside the fact that I don't belong to the subset 'you guys,' I agree," I said morosely.

"What are you going to do?"

"I'm going to have another drink," I said, waving to attract the bartender's attention. "How about you?"

"Hell, yes."

We were in The Penultimate Bar in Radetzky's Hab, and through the skin of the bubble, I could see the mellow salmon-banded curve of Big Bird. Little Bird, its gigantic moon, was rising above the edge of the planet, all cratered and battered and rocky. It was quite a sight, but I wasn't in the mood.

"But that's not what I meant," Shaker continued.

"No," I said. "I know."

I'd left Ernie to keep an eye on the probe, and Karl to keep an eye on Ernie, and I'd come back downsystem to try to formulate a plan of action, but all possible scenarios kept dropping away. The more I thought about it, the more it became obvious that there really was only one option left.

"Any word on the dewline?" I asked.

"We're running diagnostics as fast as we can. But you're talking about more than a billion satellites, at last count. It's going to take a while."

"No downtime? Blackouts? Cometary perturbations?" I'd learned that last phrase a few years ago. I still had no clear idea what it meant, but it seemed to make the dewline techs think I knew what I was talking about.

"We're working back eighteen months in the records." Shaker sat back and rubbed his eyes. "So far, nothing."

"Go back further."

"Duke, mate," he said seriously, "if that thing's been in-system for a year and a half, we're toast anyway."

"We need to know how it got through," I told him. "We need to know if there were more of them. Ernie really fucked up when she fired on it; if it had some kind of newfangled stealth coating or something, it'll have boiled away."

"Oh dear," he said.

I collected two bulbs of whiskey sour from the bartender. "'Oh dear' about covers it, yes."

"No," he said. "The boss is here."

I looked over at the doorway. "I'm your boss," I told him.

"Not while she's here, you're not."

"You're fired."

We both watched Connie somersault languidly through the doorway, looking around the bar. She saw us, kicked off a support column, and landed neatly in the seat next to us. It was beautiful to watch; I'd have injured half a dozen people and crashed into most of the decor if I'd tried that.

"I was just in your office," she said, snapping her fingers at the bartender. "Lovely office. Really great furniture and fittings. Lacking something, though. I wonder what it could be? Hm . . ." She made a show of thinking. "Oh yes," she said finally. "That's what it's lacking. You."

"I've been rousted from bed and I've been dragged up-system and back again and I'm not in the mood, Connie," I told her.

She looked at Shaker. "Now I know *you* have work to do."

Shaker nodded. "Yup." He undid his seat restraints, pushed off gently, and rose unsteadily into the air. Shaker hadn't been in the Colony very long, and one of the reasons I liked him was that he was no more adept at freefall than I was. He bumped into a couple of people and drifted off towards the exit.

"We were having a meeting," I said when he had gone.

"You were having a drink," she said, taking her own bulb from the bartender. "And I don't like you hanging around with him."

"Shaker's okay."

"He's mundane."

"So am I."

She snorted. "No you're not."

"Yes I am," I said. "And I don't like being told who I can drink with, actually."

Normally, the tone of my voice just bounced right off Connie, but this time she looked at me and shrugged. "You shouldn't drink with subordinates," she mused.

"*You're* doing it."

She gave up, which was unusual for Connie. "Okay. Fine. Drink with whoever you want. Any ideas?"

"*Whom*ever."

"Don't push your luck, Duke. What do we do?"

"I'm still thinking."

She looked at me.

"We might not *need* to *do* anything," I said. "That probe's a heap of junk; it's been popping in and out of target systems for decades. The Bureau expects to lose contact with these things eventually anyway; it barely registers when they do."

"They've already been here," she pointed out.

"Yes," I agreed. "Yes, there is that."

"So why come back?"

"Lots of possible reasons. It could be some university co-funding a one-shot mission to take a look at systems in the Bureau database. Pure research. It could be a small mining outfit paying to be part of the probe's mission profile, looking for commercially useful data."

She passed a hand over her shaven scalp. "It's not any of those things, though."

"No. It's a dangle."

She raised an eyebrow.

I sighed. "You're looking for someone," I said. "You can't be sure *where* they are, but you *can* be sure *who* they are, and if you think hard enough about it you can come up with an idea of the kind of place they *might* be. You can't physically visit all these places and check them out yourself, so what you do is send out provocations. That's your dangle. And if one of your provocations gets a response, you know you've found something worth checking out."

She blinked at me.

"The Bureau second-guessed the Writers. It's been grand-touring probes through all the systems in its database where it thinks they might be hiding, hoping that one will get shot down."

"Could still be a malf, though."

"So you send a manned follow-up to check it out. If the probe's just broken down or hit something, no harm. On the other hand . . ."

"How long?"

I shrugged. "With the latest motors they have? If they come from Nova California? Fifteen months." I saw her relax fractionally and said, "The Bureau has *thousands* of manned assets in transit at any one time. They drop out of hyperdrive at five-day intervals to make contact with base because the Bureau's terrified of losing them. That's why their ships take so long to get anywhere. All it takes is for one of them to drop out within striking distance of us and get retasked. There's no telling when they could get here. For all we know, they're insystem right now."

"The dewline would tell us."

"The dewline didn't spot the probe, and I was talking to Shaker about that when you muscled in."

She ignored that. "Dammit," she said. "We did this once before, you know, before you arrived. We lost two habs; we never did find them."

"I know," I said, although I thought *lost* was a relative term. For all anyone knew, the populations of those habs had taken a snap vote and elected to use the opportunity to strike off and set up their own colony.

"It was early on; the tech hadn't settled yet, we were still jumpy and unsure of ourselves. We did a proper check of the data afterwards," she went on, looking up at the ceiling of the bar. "There'd been a glitch, made the dewline think we were under attack. We lost forty thousand people, all because of a few crappy lines of code." She looked at me. "We can't do that again, Duke."

"No," I said. "And it's my responsibility, anyway."

———

I was having dinner in a restaurant on Angel's Rest when a very tall woman came over and sat down opposite me.

It was ice-storm season and Probity City was battened

down for the duration. I'd walked out on my job and was gradually burning my way through my savings in a slow drift through the Colonies. I'd spent a year or so with the mining operation in Gliese 581c's asteroid belt, a few months on Holden's Landing, and I'd had the misfortune to arrive on Angel's Rest just as the weather went into its regular decade-long overdrive. Now I was stuck here, watching the figures of my bank balance unspooling and considering going into suspension until the weather calmed down and the ground-to-orbit shuttles were able to take off again. What I shouldn't have been doing was sitting in the expensive restaurant of my expensive hotel and eating an expensive meal. The food was outstanding, though.

I'd just started on my main course when the very tall woman came in. Every head in the place turned in her direction. She was very nearly three metres tall, slim as a willow, stunningly beautiful, and bald as a coot, and she was wearing a clean but much-patched and repaired set of olive-green coveralls. She looked around the restaurant for a few moments as if looking for someone, then she came over to my table, pulled out the chair opposite me, and sat down and folded her hands in her lap. She looked mildly amused about something.

We looked at each other for a few moments, then one of the waiters came over and offered her the menu, but she waved it away. "I'll just have an espresso, thanks all the same," she told him.

"I'm afraid madam will have to order food if she wants to remain in the restaurant," the waiter said.

She stared at him. Even sitting down she was almost as tall as he was. Then she reached out and grabbed a couple of breadsticks from the glass in the middle of the table. She crunched one and grinned at the waiter. "Espresso, thanks," she said, and after another moment he backed away.

I went back to my Kobe beef.

After a minute or so, she said, "I watched your press release. *Very* funny."

"I'm eating," I said.

She noisily ate another breadstick until it annoyed me enough to make me look up from my meal.

"What makes a man like you quit a job like that?" she pondered, tipping her head to one side.

"If you've seen the release, you'll have a good idea."

She shrugged. "It was a good job, too. Lots of mucky-mucks in the BoC, but not that many *high* mucky-mucks."

"I'm not talking to the Press," I told her evenly. "I thought I made that clear."

"Oh, I'm not the Press," she said brightly. "I'm not even a groupie—and you do have your fair share, Mr.

Faraday. I'm here to offer you a job."

"I don't want a job."

She grinned. "Oh, c'mon, Duke—can I call you Duke?—everybody wants a job."

"I don't."

"Well you can't keep eating that stuff forever, then," she said, nodding at my plate. "Man with expensive tastes and no job, that's trouble."

"I'll manage."

She leaned forward and clasped her hands together on the tabletop. "What if I were to offer you a way to do more than just *manage*? What if I were to offer you the chance to be part of a great adventure?"

"I'm really trying to have a quiet life, Ms. . . ."

"Lang. Conjugación Lang." She smiled at me and lowered her voice until only I could hear her. "What if I were to offer you a way off this howling nightmare of a planet? Right now?"

"You have some kind of magic spaceship that takes off through seven-hundred-kilometre-an-hour blizzards?"

She wrinkled her nose and grinned coquettishly. "Oh, I have something better than that."

Probity City's spaceport was ringed with underground hangars, and in one of them nestled a little insystem tug, rough and blocky and unsubtle, covered in propulsion nozzles and tetherpoints and battered industrial tech.

"Very funny," I said. I had finished my meal and then, at Conjugación Lang's suggestion, packed what passed for my luggage and followed her down here, two hundred metres below the wind-scoured tundra of the spaceport.

Standing beside me, she nodded. "Good, isn't it?"

The words *Something Better Than That* were sprayed on the side of the tug in Comic Sans, which really was the least of the little vehicle's problems. It looked as if it could barely get off the ground on a calm midsummer's afternoon, let alone reach orbit in the middle of an ice storm.

I turned to go, but she put a hand on my arm. It was a strong hand. She squeezed gently and I felt a thrill of panic. The Bureau was, in general, too smart and frankly too busy for petty score-settling, but I'd included a couple of *ad hominem* comments in my press release and the people I'd made them about were vindictive little bureaucrats who couldn't sleep at night unless they had come out on top during the day. I'd probably been responsible for some sleepless nights.

I said out loud for the benefit of the cameras in the hangar, "I claim political asylum."

Lang looked down at me and beamed. "Bless you, Duke, I don't work for the Bureau, this isn't a kidnapping, and I spoofed all the cameras when I first got here. Nobody knows we're here but us." Her expression became serious. "Look. Just hear me out. If you still don't want to come, I'll bring you back and nobody will be any the wiser."

"You're crazy and I want to leave," I told her. But she didn't let go of my arm. Cameras or not, I was faced with the choice of having a fight with a very tall bald woman, or doing what she wanted. I said, "I'm a lawyer. What on earth do you want with a lawyer?"

She bugged her eyes out at me and licked her lips. "Never eaten a *lawyer* before."

"Look at my face," I said. "Look at my face while I scream in terror."

She let go of me. "What you did, that took stones," she said. "Not the quitting—anyone could have done that. Quitting *and* publicly criticising the Bureau like that, that's unusual."

Some years previously, a group of colonists had died while in suspension on their way to one of the newer settled worlds. Their families had brought a suit against the Bureau, and I had been one of many, many Bureau lawyers defending it. I hadn't actually come to any great liking for any of the individuals involved, but there had been instances of sharp practice involved in assembling our defence with which I was not in the slightest bit comfortable.

I'd taken my concerns to my superiors, who immediately slapped me down and suggested that I take a week or so off to think over my position, without pay.

Now, I was a grown-up and I knew the road. I was at least self-aware enough to know that the world was not perfect and that monolithic entities such as the Bureau of Colonisation always get their way, and I was realistic enough to realise that either you get on board or you get bulldozed. It was, therefore, still something of a mystery to me why, after a couple of days mooching around my apartment, I had found myself drafting a letter of resignation and a press release which made me, for an hour or two, one of the most recognisable faces on Earth.

My departure and whistleblowing had not affected the case at all, but it had made me feel better. Not particularly heroic or righteous, but better about myself, which counts for a lot sometimes. It had not made me feel in any way special or valuable.

I said, "Other lawyers are available."

She laughed. "We don't want a *lawyer*, Duke, although

a lawyer might come in handy from time to time. No, we want *you*. Now. Want to take a ride?"

I sighed. "Lead the way."

We cycled through the tug's little airlock—there was just barely room for us both—and into the cramped control room. Lang sat down in one of the control couches and started punching buttons and waking up displays.

"Sit down, Duke," she told me.

I stood where I was, my tote slung over my shoulder, genuinely curious about a number of things. Firstly, whether the tug could actually take off at all. Secondly, how it was going, as she claimed, to get into orbit when it was a basically non-aerodynamic shape which would be flying through a storm of hail powerful enough to turn a skyscraper into an eroded stump. Thirdly, how she was planning to take off when spaceport control would have to open the doors at the end of the hangar which connected it with the tunnel leading to the surface. This was, I decided, going to be one of the shorter trips I had taken.

"Well, you might want to hang on to something, then," she said.

I didn't move.

She shrugged irritably. "Okay," she said. "I gave you fair warning." And she typed a couple of commands and I was falling.

I flailed my arms and legs and windmilled in mid-air, my inner ear refusing to process anything that made any sense. I threw up my expensive dinner, and it became a big sphere of vomit that drifted swiftly across the cabin, hit a bulkhead, and exploded into hundreds of smaller spheres of vomit. I threw up again.

"Oops," said Lang. "Well, you can't say I didn't tell you so." She reached up and snagged my belt and pulled me down until I could grab on to one of the armrests of the vacant control couch and strap myself in. She, meanwhile, was jackknifing expertly out of her own couch and unclipping a hose from a cupboard to vacuum up my dinner.

I sat panting in the control couch, my balance going haywire. And then I saw the centre display on the control panel and for a moment I forgot about everything.

We were in orbit.

Angel's Rest hung in the display, a great dirty white ball of cloud. One side of it was dimpled by dozens of depressions where ice tornadoes tracked back and forth across the uninhabited Western Continent, a place so truly awful that no one had bothered to give it a name. There were plans to build great underground arcologies there one day, but that was something for the far future because for eleven months of the year it was literally impossible to travel anywhere in the west.

That there were people here at all was due mainly to a number of coincidences. The Bureau's policy regarding exploration was to make it as cost-effective as possible; it used telescopes in Earth's cometary halo to identify stars with exoplanets, then sent unmanned probes to them for a closer look. There were a lot of alien solar systems out there, so the probes usually had an itinerary running into the hundreds, and each initial probe was tasked for a simple fast-flyby, a snapshot of rocky worlds and gas giants and asteroid belts, with a special focus on any planets within the liquid-water band of that particular sun.

Stars with likely looking worlds—roughly Earth-sized rocky bodies within the liquid-water belt—got a second visit. The second wave of probes were tasked to stick around longer and do a proper survey of the system, but they were programmed with *if/then* loops—*if* the planet has an atmosphere *then* conduct a spectroscopic analysis; *if* the planet has no atmosphere *then* move on to the next target, that kind of thing—and that sort of programming is open to all kinds of errors.

In the case of Angel's Rest, the second probe arrived near the beginning of the planet's temperate phase. It found a rather chilly but still habitable world at the outside edge of the liquid-water zone—but Earth is in a similar position, and nobody's ever complained about that—with a breathable atmosphere. It finished its tests, transmitted them back to base, and moved on.

The Bureau was under a bit of pressure in those days to start living up to its name and actually come up with a colonisation programme, and what they did next was cut some corners. The Bureau's keywords when considering a planet's suitability as a colony were *environmental impact*. Here, there was no problem. The highest form of animal life was a little smaller than a rabbit and lived in enormous burrow-colonies deep underground, and the most advanced form of plant life was an insanely tough and hardy hedge-thing that grew in sheltered places. People could live here without worrying about displacing native species. It was perfect. The Bureau filled up a transport with colonists and sent them on their way.

The efficiency of the hyperdrive motors back then being what they were, the colonists arrived just after the beginning of the *next* temperate phase, and the moment they were settled and had time to look around they realised that their new home was going to get a bit cold and windy in about fifteen years' time. Instead of withdrawing the colony, which would have been a huge PR disaster, the Bureau funnelled resources into helping the colonists survive the coming ice-storm season. Half of them died anyway, which was the aforementioned huge PR disaster, but the survivors said something like, "Fuck it, we're not going to let *this* place beat us," and they were so well-prepared by the time the next hyperweather came along that nobody died. Angels were, by common agreement, some of the craziest people in the known universe.

Lang finished hoovering my sick out of the air and strapped herself back into her control couch. She looked over at me and grinned. "Good, innit?" she said.

"You can't go into hyperdrive inside a gravity well," I said calmly. "The motors won't work."

"Ah." She tapped the side of her nose with a fingertip. "I have magic motors."

"No you don't."

She chuckled. "So. Have I impressed you?"

I burped, tasted sick, heaved, managed to keep what was left of my stomach contents where they were. I said, "Will you tell me how you did that?"

"No," she said. "But I will take you to someone who will. Not that it'll do you any good; only about four people understand it."

I said, "Ms. Lang—"

"Connie."

"Who do you work for, Connie?"

"Have you ever heard," she said seriously, "of Isabel Potter?"

———————

The Writers lived all the way across the system, which with the latest generation of hyperdrive motors took less time to reach than typing the destination coordinates into the navigation computer. It took me longer to sit down in the control couch of *One Potato, Two Potato* and do up the harness.

The Writers lived in a hollowed-out rock tucked away in the system's pathetically modest asteroid belt. *One Potato* was a considerably smaller rock—most of our ships were hollowed-out asteroids of varying sizes—and we approached the Writers' vessel like a pebble nudging up against Manhattan. There was a tunnel hidden away in the bottom of one of the many craters on the rock's surface, near the axis at one end; we dropped smoothly into it and emerged in a cavern the size of an aircraft carrier, its tiered walls ranked with hundreds of tugs and ships. I found *One Potato* a space on one of the ledges, landed us, and floated through the docking tunnel into another, rock-walled tunnel.

As I drifted through the tunnel I felt my inner ears start to assign an *up* and a *down*, the rock's rotation providing a semblance of gravity that grew stronger and stronger and drew me down to the tunnel's floor and was eventually enough for me to bounce along. It was only a sixth of a gee or so, but after months in freefall I felt heavy and sluggish.

The tunnel split into two, and then into two again, and again. I kept to the left-hand fork every time, passing side tunnels full of transport containers and powered-down machinery, and bounced along in this way for a couple of kilometres until I came to a rack of bicycles. Cycling in a sixth of a gee of centripetal gravity can be tricky, but I only fell off a couple of times before I reached my destination, a little vestibule walled with Doric columns cut out of native stone, with a simple plain archway on the other side.

I stepped through the archway and out onto short-cropped grass. Before me was a landscape of gently rolling wooded hills and grasslands that faded off into a misty faery distance. To either side, the landscape curved gently away until it eventually hung overhead, obscured by the daylight tube that ran down the axis of the habitat. At my feet, a patch of crushed white stone led off to become a path that wandered away into the landscape. Some distance away, figures were approaching me along the pathway.

I sighed and shook my head. This was what happened when a bunch of Tolkien geeks got the power of life and death over an entire solar system, and I was almost exactly the wrong generation to appreciate it.

The line of figures moving along the white path resolved themselves into about a dozen elves dressed in silver armour and carrying bows and swords. They stopped just in front of me and their leader broke into a huge grin.

"Wotcher, Duke," he said. "Wassup?"

"Got a situation," I told him. "Need to talk to the Council."

His grin went away and he nodded soberly. "Yah, been keeping an eye on that. Council's expecting you."

"Excellent," I said, with more than a touch of irony. "Take me to your leaders."

———

Isabel Potter was the bogeyman. She was Baba Yaga, the Wicked Witch of the West. I actually once knew someone who invoked her name to make her children go to bed. She was Legend.

She'd started out as a professor of molecular biology at Princeton—bright, overachieving, cultishly popular with her students. Then she had moved into research into gene therapy for congenital conditions, and had made a breakthrough which even now was a closely guarded secret. Whatever it was, she had had the simple, glowing epiphany that the human body was infinitely—and desirably—hackable, and she had begun to hack it.

It was not a good time to be doing stuff like that. The US was being run by what was in effect a right-wing theocracy, which had banned experimentation on the human genome on ethical grounds. After a couple of years of banging her head against a brick wall, Potter had lost patience and simply gone ahead and produced what turned out to be the first of the Kids.

The experiment was a success, but word got out and Potter barely escaped ahead of various law enforcement agencies. On the run with a dozen or so of her graduate students, who would have taken a bullet for her, she finally settled in China, where there were no real qualms about experimenting on anything which took anyone's fancy, and for a decade she thrived. Word began to filter out of Beijing of some very odd variations on the human baseline.

The US authorities have long, bitter memories and they're prone to vindictiveness, and one night a SEAL team parachuted into the heavily guarded compound where Potter lived, took her into custody, and whisked her back to Washington, *pour décourager les autres*. Some of her students were killed in the operation.

The rest, fuelled by righteous anger, broke Potter

out of Federal prison, got her offplanet, and stole a Bureau colony transport by the simple expedient of boarding it and switching on its hyperdrive motors. Which would have been more than enough to win everyone involved a death sentence, probably, but there were more than forty thousand colonists already on the transport, waiting in suspension for a trip to one of the new Bureau worlds.

For more than five hundred years, Isabel Potter and her companions had been at the very top of the Bureau's Most Wanted List, and for more than five hundred years nobody had the faintest idea where they had gone.

The Council was elves and dwarves and hobbits and goblins and God only knows what all else. I hadn't read the right books or seen the right movies to be able to identify them all, but there were lots of Klingons there, too. Attending a Council meeting was like being at the Masquerade at a science fiction convention. Having founded the Colony, the Writers were mostly about having fun, and if that fun involved rewriting themselves as characters from late-twentieth-century popular culture, that was okay by me. They mostly left the Colony to run itself, which meant my contact with them was limited. Unfortunately, there were situations where, because they were, after all, the Founders, they were the final arbiters. I'd done this four or five times during my Presidency—although never for a situation as serious as this—and it was always like giving a presentation to an audience of toons.

The stadium where we held the meeting was a big grassy depression surrounded by trees. There was a little knoll at one end with a rough wooden podium on it, and there I stood with a huge infosheet behind me, doing the audiovisual thing. I showed them footage of the probe, told them what Ernie had done, spoke about the apparent failure of the dewline, my assessment of the situation. I laid out my arguments as clearly as anyone could when faced with a massed audience of elves, werewolves, orcs, vampires, ghouls, zombies, Jedi, several iterations of Tom and Jerry, Itchy and Scratchy, and Roadrunner and Coyote, assorted superheroes, too many Darth Vaders to count, and at least two colossal lions. To preserve my sanity and my dignity, I kept my eyes on the ground and talked quickly.

"It's my assessment," I finished, "that this probe represents a clear and present danger. It got past the dewline somehow, which either means the dewline itself is faulty—and we're still assessing that at the moment—or it was designed with the intent to infiltrate systems with passive perimeter defence, which suggests to me that it was looking for us." I looked up, and wondered, not for the first time, what kind of person had themselves rewritten as a zombie. I took a breath.

"You've examined the probe?" asked a Wolverine.

I sighed. There's always one . . . "As I said in my presentation," I reminded the audience, "the probe's a mess. Its main engine has made it *fantastically* radioactive. It's so radioactive that, if we were anywhere else, I'd be advising you right now to sue the Bureau for dropping it into the system."

Silence. Tough room. The Writers loved jokes, so long as it wasn't someone else making them.

I said, "Anyway. We can't get near it. In fact, to my mind it's *suspiciously* radioactive, as if it was deliberately poisoned. Also, Ernie seriously damaged it. If it was carrying stealth technology, we may never be able to reconstruct it."

"It's also old," mused one of the lions. "That design of fission motor dates back hundreds of years."

"Doesn't mean the probe's that old," said a Klingon. "As Duke says, they could have deliberately used a dirty design to stop anybody looking too closely at it."

"Why would they do that?" asked an elf.

"To stop us seeing what kind of stealth tech it's using," said the Klingon. "*Duh.*"

"Fuck off," said the elf. "It was a reasonable question."

Someone else disagreed. Then someone else disagreed with *them*, and all of a sudden everyone was shouting. I sighed. I'd been here a little over a century and if I had learned nothing else in all that time, it was that very very bright people just love to argue.

I raised a hand for quiet. When that didn't work, I found a gavel on a shelf under the podium and banged that for a while. When that didn't work either, I shouted, "Excuse me!"

That lowered the general volume in the amphitheatre enough for me to start banging the gavel again with some expectation of being heard, and little by little the arguing stopped.

When I had everyone's attention again, I said, "Notwithstanding the probe's radioactive state and the uncertainty of whether it contains stealth and/or surveillance technology, my assessment is that we should look very seriously at enacting Option One."

Complete silence.

I looked out over the expectant faces and I said, "We all knew this was a possibility. The Bureau has never given up looking for us. That's why we *have* Option One.

I'm not saying this lightly. I really think we're in trouble this time."

More silence.

Finally, a voice said from near the front of the crowd, "Thank you, Mr. President. We'll go away and discuss the issue."

"Okay, I said. Thank you."

"Could I have a private word with you, though?"

I felt a thrill of expectation. "Sure."

There was a little bower behind the amphitheatre. The person who joined me there was still recognisably human. She was slim and elegant and red-haired and she seemed to be in her midthirties, but you had to constantly remind yourself that nothing in the Colony was how it seemed.

"Mr. President," she said.

"Professor Potter," I said. "Nice to meet you finally."

She smiled. "If I went around personally greeting every new arrival I'd never get anything done."

"It's okay," I told her. "I've only been here a century." And it wasn't as if there was a constant stream of tourists passing through the Colony.

There were a couple of sunloungers on the grass on the other side of the bower. Potter sat down on one and motioned me to sit beside her.

"You do appreciate what you're asking us to consider

doing," she said when I was seated.

"As I told you, I'm not suggesting it lightly. I showed my working out as well as I could; can *you* think of another course of action?"

"Collapsing the habs, loading the populace into ships, going somewhere else."

"Professor, I think it's more than likely that the Bureau has *found* us. We can't fight them. We have to at least think about making a run for it."

"Can't we?" she pondered. "Fight them, I mean?"

"Well, yes, we can," I allowed. "But there are always going to be more of them than us, with more resources. If we resist they'll eventually just stomp all over us. Lots of people will get hurt."

"I could just give myself up, go quietly."

"With respect, you don't really mean that."

She chuckled sadly. "No," she said. "No, I don't." She looked about her. "I'm rather flattered they're still looking, to be honest. It's been five hundred years."

"For all they know, you've been on a ship with really inefficient motors the whole time," I told her. "Also, they'll want the colonists back."

She looked at me coolly. "You really are rather insubordinate, aren't you," she said.

"Yes, I am."

"I'm rather sorry we didn't meet earlier."

Because most of them had rewritten themselves so radically, it was quite easy to forget how old the Writers actually were, but Potter had remained more or less baseline human, on the outside, anyway. She might have been the oldest person in the galaxy; she had spent much of the first couple of hundred years of her exile in hyperdrive, fleeing through the night on not very efficient motors, but for the last three hundred years she had been here. She looked about thirty, coolly beautiful, but there was something about her eyes that I couldn't quantify, something agelessly *capable*. She was actually a little scary.

"How do you think the vote will go?" I asked.

"The vote? Oh, that's a foregone conclusion." She sighed. "We're going to fold our tents and light out for the Territories. It's a shame, but as you said, we knew this was coming sooner or later."

"I'm going to need a lot of resources and manpower."

"So are we. Option One originally called for a phased and orderly withdrawal to the first Rendezvous Point within six months of enactment. That was when the Colony was a lot smaller."

"I need to be sure I can trust the dewline," I said. "If the Bureau do enter the system and we don't spot them, it won't matter how orderly the withdrawal is. I need to make that a priority."

"We lost two habs the last time we moved," she reminded me.

"I know."

"I won't let that happen again. These people trust me—they trust *us*, Mr. Faraday. They're here because they believe in what we're doing, and they rely on us to make the right decisions. I will *not* let them down."

"With respect, Professor, this conversation is all very well sitting here in a great fuck-off big colony transport that can pop out of the system at a moment's notice, but there are over fourteen thousand, ships, tugs, and assorted transport solutions out there. Maybe half of them are hyperdrive-capable. I need to recall them all to their nearest hab. That's by far the simplest part of Option One, and that alone is going to take us weeks. Months, maybe." And that didn't take into account the dickheads who would decide that they wanted to stay behind. "And I can't give you any reasonable read on security until I can trust the dewline."

"I'll make sure you have all the manpower and resources you need, Mr. President." She stood up. "But as soon as I need them for the withdrawal, I'm taking them back." She looked down at me. "Fair?"

It was the best I could have expected, under the circumstances. "Yes. Fair."

She smiled. "You've done well; I'm proud of you. Now, we all have a lot of work to do. I want daily reports—hourly, if the situation changes."

"Of course."

"With any luck we might be able to get out of here without anyone ever being sure we were here in the first place."

"You don't believe that any more than I do."

She looked a little sad. "No," she said. "I don't."

————————

The Colony's solar system was a pile of junk, and that was why we lived there. About five hundred years ago, a fast-flyby probe had stormed through the system. It had taken snapshots of the two little rocky planets, the single gas giant with its single huge moon, the cometary halo, and then headed on to the next star on its target list.

A century later, a second probe came through for a more leisurely stay. It saw that the rocky worlds were dead; their molten cores had cooled millions of years ago, their magnetospheres had dwindled to nothing, and the solar wind had patiently, molecule by molecule, blown whatever atmosphere they'd ever had off into space. The gas giant was barely large enough to be worthy of the name, its soupy methane atmosphere worthless for commercial scoop-mining—there were easier places to find methane. The cometary halo was sparse and low in useful minerals. The probe finished its tour and dropped into hyperdrive, on its way to the next stop on its itinerary.

The system was, for the Bureau's purposes, useless. Nobody could live on the planets—even the Bureau preferred their colonies to have an atmosphere of *some* kind—and it was too low in resources to make it commercially viable for mining.

The Bureau saw junk. The Writers saw the Promised Land.

They arrived about three hundred years ago in their hollowed-out asteroid, guided by data stolen from the Bureau of Colonisation's database, and they looked about them and saw much to be pleased about. The Bureau had assessed the system in terms of either colonisation or a long-term resource-realisation operation, and by those measures it was a bust, too much trouble for too little return. But the Writers were thinking along the lines of an indigenous population of maybe a couple of million, and on that scale the Colony was a land of plenty. And the Bureau had already been here, dismissed the system, and moved on. They were statistically unlikely ever to come back.

I only discovered much later that our sudden departure from the hangar beneath Probity City's spaceport had left a tug-sized vacuum. The sudden drop in pressure as the air in the hangar rushed to fill the vacuum had caused a massive implosion, which had collapsed the little cavern. No one had been hurt, but because of Connie's infiltration of the spaceport's systems there was no record of *Something Better Than That* ever having been there, and the authorities were still scratching their heads over what had happened.

She had, I realised, never intended to take me back. There was nowhere to take me back *to*. It was going to be almost thirty years before anyone could land on Angel's Rest again, unless *Something*'s navigation systems and magic hyperdrive motors were of such exquisite accuracy that they could deposit the tug into an empty underground hangar not much larger than itself.

"Ach, I'd have left you *somewhere*, Duke," she said when I asked her about it. "Capel Dean's nice, this time of year."

I strongly suspected this was bullshit, but I kept it to myself.

It took *Something Better Than That* four days to make the crossing from Angel's Rest to the destination which Connie refused to divulge to me. With the most up-to-date motors then in existence—and I really had to doubt that *Something* had anything approaching standard motors—that would have been a trip of about ten light-years. If you factored in time dilation, for an outside observer it would have taken us the better part of a year. For me, it was four days in zero-gee, crammed into a space far too small with a person who was already much too tall for comfort, and it seemed to last a lot longer than a year.

I'd expected us to pop out at our destination within easy fusion-drive-reach of a planet, but instead all the displays showed when we arrived was blackness scattered with stars, and one slightly larger, slightly brighter star at the centre.

"Patience, Duke," Connie said when she saw the mixture of bafflement and annoyance on my face. "Patience. Magic's happening."

And then something slid into view on the displays.

It looked like a colossal Christmas tree bauble, a great translucent green sphere the size of Rhode Island, glowing from within. Through its triple-skinned surface, I could see dim green shapes, things moving about. It was like looking into a dirty aquarium.

They couldn't agree on what to call it, so they just called it "the Colony." It consisted of thirty habs of varying sizes, the Writers' stolen transport, and countless little insystem tugs and ships. The Writers had come here and found that it was good, and had proceeded to put down roots.

The first thing they did was produce the second generation of Kids—the first generation had been left behind on Earth, doomed to die in captivity as lawsuits about who they belonged to crawled through the courts and inquisitive scientists found it impossible to keep their itchy fingers off them. The Kids were superbrights, tall, fragile children with towering IQs and a penchant for terrible jokes. They were force-grown through a brief childhood and briefer adolescence, and then let loose to play around with Professor Potter's work and other, even more esoteric, stuff.

Time passed. Generations of Kids came and went—they had short, brilliant lives. The Writers—Potter and her students and their hangers-on—rewrote themselves into ever more fantastical forms. Some of them could survive in vacuum. They woke up the colonists they'd stolen and explained the situation to them. They invited them to stay, but said the ones who wanted to return home would be put back into suspension, loaded onto a ship, and left in orbit of one of the more remote colonies, the ship's navigation system carefully trashed so as not to lead the Bureau back to the Colony. Some wanted to go back, but most elected to stay and join in the Great Adventure.

By the time Connie brought me here, the Colony was a mature and functioning enterprise the Bureau would have been insanely proud of, had it not been founded by wanted criminals carrying out proscribed experiments. The population had swollen to around the optimal two million mark, the majority of them startlingly different from the human norm, for reasons practical or satirical or simply because they *could*. The Writers kept Writing. By now, it was as easy for them to alter the genome of a life form as it was for the rest of us to jot a shopping list. Later generations of Kids were so smart that they made their earlier cousins look a little slow by comparison. They started to unpick the edges of some of the fundamental questions about the Universe, developed new, clean power sources. To my continual regret, artificial gravity was not among their inventions.

To be honest, living among very very bright people could be a total pain in the arse. Leaving aside the ego-niggling certainty that I could visit any hab, throw a rock, and be virtually guaranteed to hit someone whose IQ was some frightful multiple of mine, the bastards wouldn't stop arguing.

In any other society you could go to one of your friends and say, "Hallo, mate, do you fancy going to (location *y*) and doing (activity *z*)?" and the chances are the answer you'd get would either be, "Sure, that sounds like fun," or "Sorry, sunshine, I'm busy/low on cash/can't be bothered."

Here, the answer was more likely to be, "But we can't do (activity z) because (result w or x) might occur."

To which—and I'd heard more of these conversations, down the years, than I cared to remember—the response would be, "No, (result w) cannot occur until (conditions j and m) have been fulfilled."

And you'd hear, "(Condition m) cannot be fulfilled until (event t) has occurred."

And on and on and on.

It wasn't that the Kids were bad people, especially. They were just hardwired to see all the angles of a situation, all at once, in nitpicking detail. Some of the early generations had been shy, borderline Asperger-ish, but most of the more recent ones were fully socialised and you could have a normal conversation with them, even though you knew that, in their heads, they were simultaneously analysing all the possible outcomes. It could be a bit spooky, if you let it get to you.

When the Writers, bless them, saw these character traits emerging in their children, they realised that the Colony was in trouble. The stolen colonists who had chosen to remain were enthusiastically embracing all forms of rewriting and leaping off beyond human norms. Half the time, the Kids couldn't decide *what* to do because they were too busy thinking through all the possibilities. They needed mundanes.

After giving me a tour of the Big Hab and introducing me to a couple of the Kids—who just giggled at me and talked to each other in a language they'd made up—Connie's pitch was simple. The Colony was, by any stretch of the imagination, a success, but from time to time it needed new blood, new talent, new perspectives. There was a danger of it becoming static, stagnant. So occasionally talent-spotters were sent out to do a tour of the Settled Worlds looking for likely recruits. In the middle of one such tour, Connie had caught up with my resignation press release and something about it had appealed to her sense of humour.

Join us, she told me. All the Writers want is to be left alone to do their thing—their thing which, incidentally, has cured cancer and hundreds of diseases and extended the human lifespan by several times. When they're ready they'll got back to the Settled Worlds and hand over their miracles and everyone will see that what they did was necessary for the good of the Human Race. But until then, they need to work uninterrupted.

"And if I say no?"

She shook her head. "The Writers have developed a technique that erases specific memories. It's completely foolproof. We'll just wipe everything that happened since you sat down in that restaurant on the Rest, put you into suspension, and drop you off on one of the Settled Worlds. No one will be any the wiser."

I must have looked unconvinced because she went on cheerfully, "Come on, Duke. What have you got to go back to? Celebrity's got a short half-life. Nobody will ever employ you again after the noise you made leaving the Bureau, and your savings won't last forever. You're just going to drift until you can't afford to drift any more, and then what'll you do?"

Why did I say yes? Initially it was because I had a shrewd idea that the Writers' infallible magic memory-wiping technique was accomplished with a .45 Magnum pistol round, but beyond that I had a sinking feeling that she was right, and I had known it for a while. I'd burned rather more bridges than was strictly good for me, and while it had made perfect sense at the time, in the cold light of day it looked more and more like the stupidest thing I had ever done. Whistleblowers look great in the media, but be honest, would you trust one with your company's secrets?

I shrugged. "I'll give it a try."

That was more than a century ago.

I once read somewhere that only half a dozen people have the vaguest idea how hyperdrive works. That article was wrong. The figure was actually in the low fifties, and most of them lived in the Colony.

The Colony's hyperdrive research was even more closely guarded than its other secrets. With the single exception of the time Connie had kidnapped me from Angel's Rest, the Colony's upgraded ships never made contact with other inhabited systems or outsider vessels; if we did visit elsewhere—posing as outsystem traders or whatever—we used one of the Colony's fleet of ships powered by old-fashioned motors.

We did this for reasons of self-preservation. I—and I suspect everyone apart from those fifty-odd people—viewed hyperdrive as a bit of a magic trick, a sleight of hand using incomprehensible physics. There was an element of time-dilation to hyperdrive, which may have had something to do with causality or may have had something to do with quantum reality, I had no idea. Say you had a hyperdrive motor that could move a ship a light-year in a month; when you popped out at your destination, you'd find that a year had passed in the outside universe. All of this varied depending on how efficient your motors were, according to some bizarre and counterintuitive mathematical function that someone had once shown me but I was unable to comprehend. Long story short, the more efficient your motors, the faster you got from one place to the next, and the smaller the time dilation.

As soon as the second generation of Kids were old enough, the Writers had let them loose on the hyperdrive, as a kind of graduation exercise, and the Kids had rewarded them with virtually dilationless motors that would operate within a gravity well—ships that could cross a light-year of space in a week in real time and drop out in orbit of a planet.

It went without saying that no one else had hyperdrive motors that efficient. If, by some freak accident, one of our ships had fallen into the hands of the Bureau, it would have been like putting up a big sign saying GENIUSES ARE AT WORK SOMEWHERE—WATCH OUT. Which was not the point of the Colony.

Anyway, in their wanderings through the wilder meadows of physics, the Kids discovered that if you applied a certain stress to local space it would snuff out an operating hyperdrive motor like someone blowing out a candle. They called it the Punch, and a couple of hundred years later the Writers had built this capability into one of the upgrades of the dewline, which by then was a colossal globe of satellites orbiting the system at the limits of the cometary halo.

The dewline had started out as a couple of hundred

distant early warning stations scattered through local space around the Colony, but they were unreliable and a pain in the arse to keep visiting for maintenance. So the Writers had put the problem to the Kids, who came up with an autonomous self-repairing satellite about the size of a sedan chair. Research and development had brought that down to a thing a little larger than a tangerine, capable of repairing and even reproducing itself. We raided the asteroid belts of nearby uninhabited systems for raw materials and just let the little satellites go at it, and we now had a cloud of millions of them, very nearly Von Neumann machines, or as close as anyone dared let them be, at any rate. Working collectively, they could lase and mase in frightful amounts. They constantly monitored the system as far out as Newark, the pathetic little brown dwarf six light-years distant that was our nearest neighbour. They could warp space in a way that did unspeakable things to the quantum state of a hyperdrive motor, the idea being that any intruder who popped into the system wouldn't be able to pop out again.

Of course, all this was predicated on the dewline actually working, and its failure to spot the probe's entry into the system called this into question. I needed to know if it was faulty, and if so, how. Short of a colossal coincidence—somebody actually running into an intruder, the way Ernie had—there was no other way of spotting incursions. I wanted to run a test of the active defences—fire laser and maser bursts, run the Punch—but I didn't dare in case someone was watching the system.

"You'd just wind up frying a bunch of people's drives," Shaker said. "You know what it's like—you can coordinate all you want and there'll still be someone who won't turn off his motors during the test."

"That's because everyone here is so fucking smart," I muttered sourly.

He looked at me. "You look awful."

"Cheers." I raised my glass in salute, took a drink.

Shaker was as mundane as I was. He looked baseline human, but he'd been tweaked and rewritten in ways that were not immediately obvious, none of which had prevented him being endearingly scruffy. What he was not was superbright. He was a good tech, though. It was a pity he hadn't come up with any faults in the dewline yet.

"Has anyone," he ventured gently, "suggested that you might be getting the teeniest little bit *obsessed* with the dewline?"

"I'll add your name to the list."

He sighed and looked around the bar, probably scoping it out in case Connie came in again and rousted him.

He took a little matte-black sphere from his pocket and pressed it to the stickpad on the bar top. "We're performing physical sampling now," he said.

I plucked the sphere from the pad and held it up in front of my eyes. It was featureless save for a dozen or so tiny quad nozzles. I had no idea how these things worked; it was like a chimpanzee trying to understand nuclear fusion. I stuck the little satellite to the bar again and said, "This is ridiculous."

Give him credit, he didn't say "I told you so."

"We'll keep sampling as long as we can; maybe something will turn up. But don't hold your breath."

"Will the defences work?" I asked wearily. "If we need to whack someone?"

"I keep telling you, Duke," he said. "*Everything* works, as far as we can tell. It's not a fault in the dewline; that probe had some kind of stealth capability."

"Well, we're fucked, then. There could be hundreds of the fucking things in the system right now. They could have been here for *years*."

"Dude," Shaker said solemnly, "we are leaving *anyway*."

I looked at him, a number of replies going through my mind, none of them terribly polite, but in the end I could only muster the energy to say, "Yes. Yes, we're leaving anyway."

_____

We still hadn't finished running diagnostic tests when Potter decided to pull the resources she'd let me requisition. The Colony had been preparing to hightail it for almost eight months and it still wasn't ready; all the really valuable stuff—the Kids, the research and so on—had been loaded onto the Writers' ship, and they were ready to go at a moment's notice. The population of about two-thirds of the habs was also on board; it was a bit crowded and the biosphere was going to take some knocks, but everyone would survive.

Which left the other third of the population cleaning up the system. There was no point deflating the habs and carting them to the Rendezvous Point; we emptied them of everything useful and deorbited them into the sun. It was going to be easier just to fab up new ones at the other end, although it would take years to replace the kudzu. Some of the bigger buildings had their own life support systems and hyperdrive motors; those we towed out through huge slashes in the sides of the habs and prepped for flight.

"This is a bloody circus," Connie complained at one of our weekly crisis meetings. "Nobody's going anywhere; we might as well just turn ourselves in and get it over with."

I yawned and rubbed my eyes. The Writers had given me quite a few little tweaks down the years, but it had been a while since I'd had more than a couple of hours' sleep, and I was only human, mostly. I said, "I vote we give the Writers a Go."

"That's not up to us," said Karl. "Potter'll decide when she goes, nobody else."

"Makes sense to get them off-site, though," put in Ernie, who I had drafted onto the team as a punishment for starting the whole fucking mess in the first place.

I leaned forward and rested my head on the bar. With the Big Hab now evacuated and City Hall crewed up and ready to leave, Radetzsky's was one of the few habs left where we could work, and even that was mostly empty and powered-down and rather spooky. We had invaded the Penultimate and set up our comms and other gear in the deserted bar. I was going to miss the place.

"Duke?" said Connie.

"Sorry." I sat up. "What?"

She looked at me. "You should get some shut-eye."

I shook my head. "No time. Sleep when I'm dead." I blinked. "Okay. We let Potter decide. So. What next?"

"We're at ninety percent," said Shaker, meaning the interminable crawl of the dewline diagnostic. "Still no significant deterioration."

"Jesus," I muttered. "It'll be the last thing you look at; it's always the last thing you look at."

Everyone looked at me. I'd assembled the Crisis Team early on in my term as President, on the grounds that I would probably never need them but if I did, I would be too busy to put them together later. I'd sat down one evening—here in the Penultimate Bar, as it happened—with a tablet and a copy of a database the Writers had given me, and tried, Kid-like, to think about every possible disaster that could befall the Colony and which skills I would need to help me deal with them. It would have made more sense, on the face of it, to just ask a couple of the Kids to do it for me, but they would just have spent the whole time arguing and I'd still have been waiting for an answer when disaster overtook us.

I wound up with ten names, to which I added Connie's and my own for my personal Dirty Dozen. Ernie brought us up to thirteen, and we gathered in the Penultimate at least once a week and basically just bitched about the whole sorry business for a few hours until we felt sufficiently rested to go back out and start all over again. This may not have been the most efficient way to do things, but I was a lawyer, not a manager, and it wasn't my fault that this situation had happened during my Presidency.

Karl was my Vice President, a post he used mostly to get free meals in restaurants. He and I were the most mundane people I knew in the Colony. Shaker was there because he worked on the dewline. Karen von Pahlen and Ernie were upsystem miners. Bo Grant was an infrastructure specialist we'd recruited from a Bureau colony on one of the worlds of Epsilon Eridani. Reece Callaghan took care of our long-range planning. And so on. I'd spent some time casting about for the most socialised Kid I could find, on the grounds that we probably wouldn't get very far without at least one superbright, and wound up with the Twins, Turold and Telifer, who were impossible to tell apart and were basically one personality in two bodies. This could be spooky at times, but I'd learned to live with it. I'd asked Potter if one of the Writers would volunteer for the Crisis Team, but none of them could be bothered and in the end I'd dropped the subject.

Everyone was still looking at me. They all looked exhausted, and I belatedly realised that they were all waiting for me to tell them to go and get some sleep.

"Okay," I said. "Time out. Go away, get some food, get some sleep, get a shower. Back here in eight hours."

Everyone else left, but Connie stayed behind, sitting at one of the tables watching me as I scrolled through lists of stuff on my tablet. "So," I said. "Points?"

"You're doing fine, Duke," she told me. "You could maybe learn to delegate a bit more."

"Delegate? I'm practically running this thing from a Jacuzzi as it is."

She chuckled. "You put together a good team."

"More by luck than judgement."

"You put together a good team," she insisted gently. "They know what they have to do, and they're good at it. It's just the . . . the *scale* of the thing."

I looked up from the tablet. "Do you think I was right?" I asked. "To recommend Option One?"

"I don't know. I do think I'd prefer not to be here when we find out whether you were right or not."

"No word from Earth?"

"No word from anywhere. Which doesn't mean anything."

"Quite." Like any other small, embattled, and basically paranoid nation, we had spies in the enemy camp, mundanes recruited by Connie and others and then run back into the Settled Worlds to report on stuff. Some of them worked for the Bureau. In addition, we were always visiting, checking the news feeds, tasting the zeitgeist, looking for signs that would give us an early warning of the Bureau making some kind of move against us. None of those assets had been able to find any information at all about the probe, or about a larger probe project. That didn't mean these things did not exist, but it would have been nice to have some independent confirmation of my fears. I was battling a dreadful sinking feeling that we were doing this for nothing, that the probe was a one-off, but I didn't dare take the chance. We had to go.

I unstrapped myself, manoeuvred around the bar, and filled a bulb with whiskey sour. "Want a drink?"

"No, but knock yourself out. Oh, you already are. Jolly good."

"Don't."

She put on a mock-innocent face. "Don't what?"

"Just don't." I went back to my stool and strapped myself down again and took a big drink. I looked out through the huge picture window of the bar; I could just see the top curve of Big Bird, its thick atmosphere swirling and roiling with storms. There was a scoop-tanker in close orbit of the little gas giant; methane was a handy raw material for the modest needs of the Colony. If we were serious about trying to leave no signs that we were here, I was going to have to remember to either have the tanker dropped into the sun or fitted with hyper-drive motors. My brain was so fried that I couldn't decide which.

Connie was reading something on her tablet. "And

thirty people don't want to go at all?"

"Personally, I'm surprised it's not more."

"What are you planning to do with them?"

"I've had them sedated and put into suspension." I saw the look on her face. "We can't leave them behind, Connie. I'll apologise to them when we get wherever we're going."

"It's going to have to be a pretty spectacular apology."

"And it's kind of low on my list of priorities right now. Anything else?"

She turned off her pad and shook her head. She folded her hands in her lap and looked at me. "I'm worried about you, Duke."

I took another drink. "Thank you."

"Really. You do need to delegate more; you're taking too much of the weight."

"It's the only way I can be sure stuff's getting done, Connie."

"I know, but you've got to learn to trust your team. You'll be no use to any of us if you get sick."

I looked at her. "Anything else *important*?"

"When this is all over, you get a holiday. A long holiday."

"Yes," I said, looking out of the window again. "Well, we're *all* going on a long holiday really, aren't we?"

———————

In the end, it was all a bit of an anticlimax.

After months of too little sleep and too much work and too much to think about, all of a sudden there was nothing left to do, and one morning I sat in the control couch of *One Potato, Two Potato* and watched the displays as the Writers' ship popped out of the system. There was no fuss about hyperdrive, no flashing lights or sudden claps of thunder. One second the great asteroidal rock was there, the next it was gone. On its way to the Rendezvous Point.

Like everyone else in the Settled Worlds, we communicated using qubit transceivers, lattices of entangled atoms which made it possible to speak in real-time over enormous distances. I started to get qubit transmissions from the rest of the Crisis Team, scattered across the system, as they reported that the rest of the fleet had begun leaving.

It took about fifteen minutes. Then we were all alone. Thirteen souls in stealthed boats, drifting through the dark on minimum power, the last line of defence.

The final job of tidying up was the dewline. Billions of tiny orbiting satellites englobing the system might be something of a giveaway for any inquisitive Bureau ships which came looking for the lost probe, as well as coming under the heading "tech we'd rather the Bureau didn't have," so we had instructed it to eat itself.

It was basically just the same process that the satellites used to reproduce themselves. We had just reprogrammed it to consume itself and build an enormous boulder of refined minerals and metals, which we would fly to the Rendezvous Point, pick up instructions about where to go next, and fly on to the new Colony, where it would be broken down again into a new dewline.

Trouble was, this was going to take a while, and someone needed to supervise the process and make sure the Bureau didn't turn up unannounced in the middle of it all. So the Crisis Team were a stay-behind group, tasked with giving the Colony as much lead time as possible while finishing the little details of tidying up the system.

When the last of the Colony's vessels were safely away, I looked around the flight deck of *One Potato*. The ship was pretty roomy, by most standards, but I had a suspicion I was going to start feeling the walls closing in on me before it was our turn to leave.

"Okay," I said on the general channel. "Thank you, everyone, that seems to have gone smoothly. If there's nothing else, head for your assigned positions, power down, and go to sleep. I'll see you in eighty years, if every-thing works out."

There was a chorus of "Night, Duke" from the rest of the team—grudgingly in Ernie's case—and then their telemetry showed them going into suspension, one by one, until there was only Connie and myself left.

"I really didn't think we'd make it," she told me over a private channel.

"We're not out of the woods yet."

"You're just a little fucking ray of sunshine, aren't you?"

"We've been lucky so far," I said. "We still have to stay lucky for another eighty years. That's a lot to ask."

"The Colony got away," she pointed out. "They're safe. You did your job, Duke."

"I've done my job when we turn up in the new system with the dewline." I typed the strings of commands which began powering-down *One Potato*. "And we'll cross that bridge when we get to it. I'm going to turn in, Connie. Let's hope we're not disturbed, eh?"

"Yes," she said. "Sleep well, Duke. You've earned it."

———————

Coming out of suspension affects different people in different ways. I used to know someone who said it made him feel as if he was waking up with flu and the worst hangover of his life, but I've spoken to others who said they came round with no ill-effects at all and felt as if they'd just had a very long, very refreshing sleep.

I probably fell somewhere in between. When I opened my eyes, they were gummy and I felt groggy and glueymouthed, but I'd felt much worse. And besides, I had other things to worry about.

The display on the lid of my suspension unit was blinking red and there were far too many status updates. The first thing I saw was the date and time, and that was enough to tell me that things had not gone well. I'd only been asleep just over ten years; the dewline had barely had time to start disassembling itself.

The rest of the heads-up only confirmed the story. Four days ago, the dewline had detected the approach of a small object, right at the far edge of its range. Then it had lost the object. Then it had detected a small object suddenly appearing at two light-years' distance. The small object had manoeuvred for a while, then disappeared again and another small object—by this time the dewline was assuming they were all the same thing—had popped out at a light-year's distance. The object did some more manoeuvring until about two hours ago, when it had suddenly popped out and popped back in deep downsystem, just outside Big Bird's orbit. The ship gave me a menu of options. I sighed and chose the last one and watched the lid of the unit hiss open.

———

"If it's stealthed, it isn't stealthed very well," Karl muttered.

"I'm more worried about the fact that it's here at all," I said.

"There is no such thing as coincidence," said one of the Twins, Turold or Telifer, I couldn't tell the difference and it didn't matter anyway. "The Universe is basically deterministic."

"I'm inclined to agree, at least this time," Connie put in.

"It's been more than eleven years since the probe arrived," Karen noted. "That's a long time for the Bureau to sit around dithering about what to do next."

"There could be any number of reasons for that," Karl replied. He sounded like one of those people for whom emerging from suspension was a less than happy experience.

I shook my head. "The Bureau's database of surveyed systems is huge. The chances of us getting two random visitors like this is . . ." I shrugged. "I don't know."

"Well, the dewline can't get a clear read on it yet," Shaker said. "About all we can tell is that it's not very big. All that jumping about it did suggests it's not an automated probe, but the dewline's not reporting anything resembling another ship right out to the limits of its range, so it probably isn't remotely piloted."

"They could be using a qubit link to telefactor it," Reece said. "They could be piloting it from Earth."

"Not enough bandwidth," Karl said.

"A closer look might help," Connie said.

"I say we toast it right now and get the hell out of here," said Ernie. "It's already seen the dewline."

"Not necessarily," Shaker said. "Not unless it was looking or it ran into one of the satellites."

"Duke?" asked Connie.

"Technically, my term as President ended eight years ago," I told her. "I'm not running things any more."

"For shame, Duke," she said, a chuckle in her voice. "Suspension doesn't count. You know that."

"Mm hm." I muted the conference call and said, "*One Potato*."

"Yes, Duke?" said the ship's AI.

"Where's the intruder now?"

A schematic of the system popped up in one of the displays: the sun at the centre, little coloured balls and dotted lines to show the planets and their orbits, a faint ring of stardust to suggest the asteroid belt. One tiny little sapphire light glowed brightly to show where the bogey was. It was two-thirds of the way across the system from my present position.

I said, "*One Potato*, is there some way we can get close enough to that thing for a good look, without alerting it to our presence?"

"There's no way to answer that, Duke," said the ship. "I don't know how good its sensor suite is."

Fair point. *One Potato* was so effectively stealthed that it had the radar signature of a watermelon, but there was no telling what the Bureau was packing these days, industrial espionage notwithstanding.

I opened the call again. "Okay. I'm going in to have a closer look. I'll pop in with Big Bird between me and it, power down, and let my orbit bring me into visual range. How does that sound?"

The usual sounds of agreement and disagreement, over the link. Fortunately, as well as being instantaneous, qubit transmissions were impossible to intercept. Also fortunately, if I was still running the show I could ignore everyone else and just do what the hell I liked.

I typed in a couple of strings of coordinates and was gone.

The bogey was a fat cylinder about ten metres long, with a dustbin-sized white drum at one end and a weird assembly like a crown of thorns ringing the other. It had no markings, no exterior features except a line of hyperdrive pods and a few sets of manoeuvring quads.

"What's wrong with this picture?" said Karl.

"No meteor shield," said Bo. "He hits something, he's in a world of hurt."

"Could have ditched it," Karen said.

"And then what?" Bo asked. "Where's he going to get another one?"

"I've never seen anything like that before," Reece said.

"That's fucking small for a long-range ship," one of the Twins said. "It's got to have support somewhere."

"There's nothing but us as far out as Newark," said the other Twin.

"Meaningless," said Shaker. "That's close enough for backup."

"Depends how good their motors are," Karl said.

"If they haven't got our motors, it's too far away for effective backup," Reece said.

"Duke?" said Connie.

I was staring at the image on the display, illuminated by daylight reflected from the top of Big Bird's atmosphere, an itchy feeling climbing the back of my neck.

"Duke?" Connie said again.

"I don't know," I told them. "I really don't."

"Radio transmission," said *One Potato*. "He's talking."

I sighed. "Of course he is. Okay, let's see it."

The image of the intruder in the display was crowded up into a little box by the image of a small, black-haired, olive-skinned man with a neat goatee. He was wearing a clean pair of blue coveralls and behind him I could see what looked like a cluttered flight deck.

"... emergency," he was saying. "If anyone receives this, please respond. This is Simeon Bivar of the independent survey vessel *Gregor Samsa*. My hyperdrive motors have malfunctioned and my primary insystem drive has suffered an instability. This is an emergency. If anyone receives this—"

I muted the transmission. "Okay. His name's Simeon and he's in trouble. Any ideas?"

"*Kill* him," said Ernie. "Fuck it, Duke, have you never read *The Iliad*?"

"Could be kosher," I said.

"Just by accident," Ernie said. "Dropping into *my* system and having multiple malfs. Yeah, right."

"It maybe does explain his approach manoeuvres," Karen offered. "Maybe."

"Okay," I said. "Does he see us?" I was orbiting Big

Bird, close enough for the planet's pathetic magnetosphere to give me some shielding. *Gregor Samsa* was over half a million kilometres away, almost in Little Bird's orbit.

"Impossible to know," said Karl. "We don't know what he's got."

"Well *that's* no fucking help," I said.

"If he's carrying *all* the cutting-edge equipment we know the mundanes have, no, he can't see us," one of the Twins said. "But we should assume they have tech we *don't* know about, so we should assume he can see us."

"You people do my head in," I muttered. "Why are we bothering?"

"You could always ask him," Connie suggested.

"Sure," said Karl. "Like he's going to tell us he has a tactical advantage."

"We could just wait and see what he does," Karen said. "We're not in a hurry."

"If he's seen the dewline, he'll know the Writers were here," said Ernie. "We can't leave him alone, Duke."

"He wouldn't even *be* here right now if he'd found the dewline," Connie told her. "He'd have hightailed it. He'd be on his way to Nova California by now."

"I don't know, Duke," Karl said. "If he can see us, you'd think he'd run for it. But that'd give away a tactical advantage, like I said."

"It would make him a pretty cool customer, sitting there like that knowing there's thirteen ships looking at him," Karen pointed out, which I thought was the first useful piece of intelligence to come out of the whole conversation. Assumption: Simeon Bivar is a pretty cool customer.

I said, "Actually, I think there's a way I can make this work."

Silence.

"You might have a bit of fucking faith in me," I muttered.

───────────

I waited until Big Bird was between me and *Gregor Samsa*, then I popped out of the system a couple of light-years, performed a sort of three-dimensional dogleg of manoeuvres, and popped back in from another direction to within a quarter of a million klicks of the intruder.

"Is everyone listening in?" I asked.

A chorus of affirmatives.

"Okay," I told *One Potato*. "Let's talk to him."

Simeon's message popped up in the display in front of me. I said, "This is William Jefferson Clinton, of the trading vessel *One Potato, Two Potato*. I heard your message. How can I help you?"

The recording was replaced by live feed of Simeon Bivar, his face wearing a wide grin. "John Wayne Faraday," he said admiringly. "I've watched your press release."

I cut him off. "Everyone shut down," I said to the others. "I'm going to punch him. I'll see you at RP Two." And I told *One Potato* to transmit the Punch codes to the dewline.

The lights went out. The screens went dead. The aircon fell silent. I sat there in total blackness for what seemed like forever but was only a few seconds, as the Punch propagated through the system at several times the speed of light.

The lights came on. Then the consoles. Then I felt the breeze of the air circulation system on my face. I looked at the displays.

"Right," I said. "Where did he go?"

———————

The ship drew me a conference space, a cosy panelled study with a roaring log fire in the fireplace and walls lined with bookshelves. It drew a semicircle of high-backed leather armchairs in front of the fire, each one with a little mahogany side-table with a brandy snifter on it. I walked over to the window, lifted back the heavy velvet curtains. It was raining outside, and it sounded as if it was blowing a gale. The Writers had loved virtual environments even before they left Earth, and they'd set the Kids to improving and improving them and coming up with direct neural inputs, until it was impossible to tell what was real and what wasn't. It was ferociously detailed; all the books in here were different, and I could take down any one of them and read it.

The other pilots logged in one by one. Karl made a beeline for the humidor, took a cigar, and lit it with a spill from the fire. I was interested to see, when Ernie arrived, that the ship drew her without mods. She looked pretty and fresh-faced and wide-eyed, and about sixteen.

There was some small talk as everyone arrived, but when we were all settled down in our armchairs, I said, "I want to apologise for that."

"There was no way you could know he'd recognise you, Duke," Connie said. "It's been over a hundred years."

"I might still have been able to wing it, but I panicked."

"Enough, Duke. It's done now. We have to decide what to do next."

I nodded and looked at Karl, who said, "Right. Do you

want the good news or the bad news?"

I said, "I'd like all the news, thanks, Karl. As straight-forwardly as possible, please."

He chuckled. "Okay. Well . . ." He pointed, and on the chimneybreast a window appeared that seemed to open into deep space. In the middle of the window floated *Gregor Samsa*.

"Okay," said Karl. "The good news is that the mundanes haven't come up with some new stardrive or magical stealth technology. This is *Gregor Samsa* a few seconds before it disappeared." Suddenly the window was empty. "And this is *Gregor Samsa* a few seconds *after* it disappeared." He made a twirling gesture with his index finger and the intruder reappeared. "Now watch." We watched for a few seconds, then all of a sudden *Gregor Samsa* seemed to *smear* somehow. Then it was gone again.

We all looked at Karl.

"I've slowed this recording down . . . oh, a *fantastic* amount," he said. "You wouldn't believe me if I told you. That smudgy thing is *Gregor Samsa* leaving the building at an acceleration a hair over thirty-eight gees."

"From a standing start?" said Karen.

"The dewline picked up some pretty esoteric physics going on around *Gregor* when it took off," Karl told her. "It's not hyperdrive, but it might be related.

I'm still trying to figure it out. Anyway, his main motor's an antimatter torch. That was pretty straightforward to work out."

We all sat there for a while, considering this.

Karl took a drag on his cigar and said, "Let's forget about his mode of propulsion, just for a second, because there's a bigger issue here."

"The mundanes have got antimatter motors to work and there's a *bigger* issue?" asked one of the Twins, helpfully identified as Telifer by the simple expedient of *One Potato* drawing a *Te* over his head.

"There's nobody aboard that thing," Karen said. "They'd have been killed instantly."

"Unless this 'esoteric physics' protected them," Connie said.

"I'm not ruling that out," Karl said. "But the simplest explanation is that the mundanes have cracked strong AI. Simeon is a computer program."

"Bollocks," said Ernie, adding to thin air, "No offence."

"None taken," *One Potato* said out of nowhere.

Artificial intelligence—true artificial intelligence—was a fiendishly complicated thing. It made hyperdrive look like an internal combustion motor. It had taken the Kids almost two hundred years to make any breakthrough at all, and it was generally accepted that nobody in the Settled Worlds was going to get on top of it any time soon.

"It gets better," Karl went on. "I don't think the Bureau have told him what he is."

"Aw, Jesus," muttered Shaker.

Karl looked at the end of his cigar. "I think they've drawn him into a virtual environment where he believes he's a real person." He waved a hand at the conference space around us. "They can tell him anything they want; how's he going to know?"

"All of which makes *Gregor Samsa* a prize worth having," said Connie. "Antimatter drive, weird physics, strong AI." She looked at me. "If only to see what we're up against."

I sighed. "Where is he now?"

The image on the chimneybreast changed. Now it was the standard system schematic. A cluster of ruby-red dots was us, formed up at Rendezvous Point Two. The bright sapphire that was *Gregor Samsa* floated serenely on its own about fifty million klicks away.

"He's decelerated below solar escape velocity again," said Shaker. "Barely drifting along."

"The Punch obviously worked," Karen said. "His motors are dead. Otherwise he'd have popped out."

"This is so *obviously* a trap, Duke," said Ernie. "We should just kill him and get the hell out of here."

That did have a certain appeal. On the other hand, Connie was right. *Gregor Samsa* seemed to be packed with every piece of cutting-edge tech the Bureau possessed, and some of it was weird and dangerous. It needed to be examined, analysed, countermeasures devised.

We had to take Simeon Bivar alive.

———————

"That wasn't very friendly," he said. "Now my hyperdrive motors *really* don't work."

"So we're dropping all that 'ship in distress' bullshit, are we?"

He smiled, there in the display. "You're too smart for that, but it was worth a try."

"I'm not that smart. It got me to approach you."

He grinned. "You only wanted to help, Duke. Can I call you Duke? Everyone does, right?"

"My friends do, yes."

One Potato, Two Potato and *Gregor Samsa* faced each other across about fifty kilometres of empty space, talking to each other by comm laser, which, considering some of the other tech we were collectively packing, was a little like having a conversation by writing things on paper aeroplanes and throwing them at each other.

"We got off on the wrong foot," I said. "Perhaps we could have a time out and just chat for a while."

He beamed at me. "Sure. I'm not going anywhere. By the way, that's new, the thing you used to disable my hyperdrive. How does that work?"

"I'll tell you if you tell me how you can accelerate at thirty-eight gees from a standing start without your ship turning you into a greasy red smear and then disintegrating."

Simeon laughed. For a man—or a computer program which believed itself to be a man, at any rate—who thought he was stranded in a faraway system, he was in quite a good mood.

I asked, "Do you have any backup?"

He shook his head. "It's just me. You?"

I shook my head. "Just me."

He laughed again. "Come on, Duke. We're just going to sit here lying to each other all day, aren't we?"

I sighed. "There are twelve more ships around the system. Do you have any backup?"

"No, I don't."

"That doesn't sound very likely."

He shifted in his control couch. "Look, Duke," he said soberly. "Shall we start at the beginning? Full disclosure?"

The Punch would have scrambled any qubit lattices

he was carrying; he wasn't going to talk to anyone, all he could do was run away very quickly for brief periods. I said, "Okay, Simeon. Full disclosure. Did the Bureau send that probe to find us?"

He nodded. "Yes. We've been sending them out to surveyed systems for almost a century now. It's cheaper than manned missions and we can sell the extra data they send back."

Waste not, want not. "You must think we're pretty stupid."

"I think that given the choice between lying low and letting the probe leave again without knowing what it might or might not have seen, and just shooting it down to make sure, you'll shoot it down every time. The Bureau wins either way."

I scowled. "Why did it take so long to follow it up?"

"We lose more probes than you might think, just from natural wastage. Malfunctions, collisions with other bodies, stuff like that. They all have to be checked out. This system was a ways down the list."

I didn't know whether to be relieved or offended. I said, "It's been almost a decade, Simeon."

He nodded. "We're looking in *lots* of places."

"It's not just that, though, is it?" I was feeling my way around the edge of something. "It's been almost five hundred years since Professor Potter stole that boat.

Most of the ethics laws she broke were repealed centuries ago. Is she maybe not such a *priority* any more?"

Simeon's lips set in a thin, angry line. "Potter didn't just steal a ship, Duke. She's still one of the biggest mass-murderers in history. We don't forget that kind of thing, and we don't forgive."

"What are you talking about, 'mass murderers'?"

He tipped his head to one side. "Potter and her little band of madmen murdered the majority of the colonists she abducted and used the rest of them for experiments. There's no statute of limitations on that."

"Bullshit. Most of them decided to stay. We sent the rest back to you."

"Come on, Duke. Does that even *begin* to make sense?"

"It's bullshit."

"It's *history*. Documented history."

I cut the connection.

"He's lying," said Karl.

"You've seen the footage of the colonists going back," Connie said. "You've seen some of the interviews with the ones who decided to stay. I know you have, because I showed them to you when you first came here."

"Toast him," Ernie said. "Toast him and let's go find the Colony. I'm sick of this."

"He's gone again," said Shaker.

I looked at the displays, and *Gregor Samsa* was, in fact, nowhere to be seen. I sighed. "Where is he this time?"

It took the dewline a little while to locate *Gregor* again. When the little blue spark popped up in the navigation display it was almost halfway back out to the cometary halo.

"Could he actually make a run for it on his antimatter drive alone?" I mused.

"At that acceleration?" said Karl. "Sure; we can't hope to catch him. The best we could do is jump ahead of him and get in his way. That would spoil his day pretty definitively."

I sighed.

"Anyway," said Connie, "that pretty much wraps up the AI thing. He just decelerated at thirty gees; there's nothing organic aboard *Gregor*."

"We've got to whack him," Ernie said. "We can't just keep chasing him around the system until a carrier full of Marines turns up."

"Alternatively, we could just bug out now," Bo put in. "The Colony got away and that was the whole point of the exercise."

"It'll just make the Bureau look all the harder if they know we were here," Connie said. "We were hoping they'd give up one day."

"It's been five hundred years, Con," Bo told her.

"They're never going to give up."

"Also I'd really like to get my hands on that ship," Karl said. "Probe. Ship. Whatever. It's worth having for the drive alone."

I sighed again. "*One Potato*, send a message to *Gregor Samsa*. Tell him to wait where he is and I'll be over there shortly. Tell him I don't intend to fire on him or otherwise harm him. I just want to talk."

"Yes, Duke," said the ship.

"Everyone else, hang back on the other side of the system. Let's not crowd him until I've figured out what to do."

————————

I popped out of hyperdrive a respectful distance from *Gregor Samsa* and waited there, patiently transmitting friendship messages and feeling rather absurd for doing so, and eventually Simeon's image popped up on the display.

"What did you do that for?" I asked.

"You cut me off," he said. "I thought you were getting ready to fire on me. I'm not armed."

And I believed *that* about as much as I believed in Santa Claus. I said, "I was consulting with my colleagues, that's all."

He snorted. "*Colleagues*."

"We were discussing what the point was of you trying to convince me that Professor Potter killed the colonists."

"Because it's the truth?" he suggested.

"Look, Simeon, I *know* some of those colonists. They're alive and well, I promise you." Although not recognisably human anymore, but that was life in the Colony. "You've been fed a line. The Bureau's been lying to everybody."

He looked at me. "Where are your *colleagues*?"

"On the other side of the system. But they're listening in on us and they'll be here before you know it if you try something cute."

"Try something cute? You're the one who crippled my ship."

That, at least, was fair enough. I said, "How long till you're tagged as overdue and someone comes looking for you?"

"Not nearly long enough for your purposes, certainly. And anyway, if I just disappear the Bureau will suspect I found something in this system."

"We can make it look like an accident," I said in what I hoped was a threatening tone of voice.

"I'm sure you can. But they'll still be suspicious." He rubbed his face. "Doesn't matter, anyway. You'll be long gone and we'll have to start all over again." He blinked at me from the display. "Well. This is interesting, isn't it? What shall we do now? Game of Scrabble?"

"I was rather hoping you'd see sense and let us try to repair your hyperdrive."

"Why would you do that?"

"So you could go back and tell everyone the Bureau's been lying to them."

He shook his head sadly. "Duke, Duke," he said. "I can practically hear you salivating at the prospect of a look at *Gregor*'s main drive."

Personally, I couldn't have cared less about the fucking thing, aside from how complicated it was making my life at the moment. "You can't blame me for trying."

"Oh, no. No, I can't. I'd have thought a little less of you if you hadn't tried." He looked around the flight deck of *Gregor Samsa*—the simulation of the flight deck of *Gregor Samsa*—and shrugged a little.

I tried to arrange the situation in my head. Had he seen the dewline and decided to scout downsystem anyway? Had he sent a message out before *One Potato* even woke me up? Or had he popped into the system and missed any sign of habitation before I contacted him? Did it even matter? The dewline wouldn't finish tidying itself up for another seventy years or so; he'd have been declared missing and someone sent out to check on him long before then. The best thing I could do was keep him talking until I could work out how to take his ship and all its juicy tech, then hightail it. My head hurt.

I said, "Simeon, listen. I have some bad news for you."

He grunted. "My ship's fucked, I'm all alone in a hostile system, and my comms are cooked, and you have some *bad* news for me?"

"We think you're an artificial intelligence."

He stared at me for a few moments. Then he burst out laughing. Not an appreciative chuckle. Not a brief belly laugh. A flat-out, doubled-over paroxysm of laughter that left him damp-eyed and pressing a hand to his chest while he tried to catch his breath.

I said, "Your ship's about the size of a bus, Simeon. There's barely room for life support."

He wiped his eyes and chuckled. "*Gregor's* stealthed, Duke. It's *supposed* to look like that."

"That's pretty good stealth tech," I told him.

He shook his head. "Oh, that's *priceless*," he said, "*I'm* not an AI. *You* are."

"*Excuse* me?"

"I mean, they must have you running in a pretty sophisticated environment and everything, if you think you're a person," he went on. "What's it like in there? Is it nice?"

I cut him off.

"That was . . . unexpected," Karl said.

"He's hardly going to admit it," Telifer said. "He thinks he's real. He thinks anything he's been programmed to think."

"This is all getting just a little bit surreal," I told everyone.

"Kill him," said Ernie. "Just kill him. We've wasted enough time on this."

I opened the connection again.

"That was an unusual thing to say," I told Simeon.

"Says the man who just accused *me* of being an artificial intelligence."

Fair point.

He leaned forward against his harness straps. "Time to get serious, Duke. We don't have a lot of time."

"Don't have a lot of time until . . . what, exactly?"

"I'm going to send you an image from my cameras. Will you accept it?"

"I'll look at it; I can't tell you whether I'll *accept* it."

"Okay. Here it comes."

One Potato sandboxed the image, made sure it wasn't carrying any nasty computer-related weaponry, and put it up on the display. It was a picture of a rock studded with thruster quads, hanging in space. It looked a little like *One Potato, Two Potato*, but if the quad nozzles were anything to go by it was too small. Much too small.

"Your *Writers*—yes, I know that's what you call them, we'll get to that in a moment—have been popping into uninhabited systems for almost five hundred years," Simeon was saying. "They seed them with a bunch of Von Neumann machines that form a defensive grid, and then they move on."

My head really was hurting; it was turning into a thudding headache. "Why?"

"Because they're *crazy*, Duke. Potter and her pals are stone-cold crazy. They've got a grudge against the Bureau and they've decided to take their revenge by denying systems to us. Sometimes it's systems like this, not worth much at all. But sometimes it's useful, habitable systems. We've lost ships to the things they leave behind. Not probes. Ships. Full of real people. And every time we look for those lost ships, we find a shell of microsatellites around the system. And we find you."

"Me?"

"The dewline—and yes, we know you call it that too—has massive computing power, collectively. That's where you live, that's what's hosting your environment. I'm going to send you some video now, okay?"

"Okay."

"Two hundred years ago a . . . a dissident, I guess you'd call her, turned up on Bellerophon. Bellerophon doesn't owe the Bureau any favours, but when they saw what she was carrying, they got in touch. She said she'd had a change of heart, decided to make a run for it. Maybe she did; maybe she just had an argument with Potter, we never got to the bottom of it because she died. Potter and her friends had tweaked everyone so that their immune system relied on a certain genetically engineered substance only found in their travelling circus. Without it, the dissident's immune system crashed and she died."

I stared at him.

"She brought out some footage, which is what made Bellerophon contact the Bureau. And this is it. Here it comes now."

It was hard to watch, for lots of reasons.

It was the Colony. Or a colony like the Colony, anyway, and yet completely different. The first sequence was an approach to a hab, except that where the Colony's habs were huge green-tinted Christmas tree bubbles this one was tiny and a mucky brownish colour, the tough outer skin almost opaque. It looked diseased.

The next sequence was inside the hab. There was obviously something wrong with the life support system; the air was thick and soupy and full of condensation. Instead of kudzu, the structural members were construction coral, and they were dripping with algae or mould or something, as if the polyp itself was sick. But that wasn't the worst thing.

People drifted past the camera's viewpoint. Painfully thin, etiolated people. Most of them were naked or just wearing scraps of clothing. They looked grey and listless, their skin covered with sores. They were obviously suffering from a bunch of deficiency diseases.

The scene cut to a poorly lit rocky cavern. I couldn't make out how large it was, but it faded away into a dim distance. The floor of the cavern was littered with makeshift huts and benders constructed from bits and pieces of equipment—plastic sheeting, sections of panelling. More sick people drifted by.

"This is the ship Potter and her friends stole," Simeon said. "Their very own slum in the sky."

The scene cut again, and this time I had to stifle a shriek.

The creature in the image looked barely human. Its head was three or four times too large for its matchstick body and it was writhing weakly against the straps that held it down in a heavily customised control couch. Wires and tubes led from its body to various pieces of cobbled-together-looking machinery on the floor around the couch.

"According to the dissident, this is one of Potter's

superbrights," Simeon said. "Looks like she still hasn't quite got the hang of this genetic modification thing, eh?"

Someone moved into the shot, and the camera pulled back to accommodate her. She was small and dreadfully obese and wearing what might once have been a lab coat over a tattered pair of coveralls. Her skull was misshapen and a few bits of white hair still adhered to it. Her face was deeply lined, her eyes rheumy, and she moved, even in the microgravity, with all the difficulty of a terminal arthritis sufferer. She did something to one of the machines—her knuckles were like handfuls of walnuts—and then stepped aside again, and the creature on the couch began to babble strings of numbers.

"Potter herself," Simeon said. "She's obviously found a way to extend the human lifespan, but equally obviously it's not a hundred percent effective. We think she's using the superbrights as computing engines on some kind of project; they appear to have made some breakthroughs, down the years. None of them particularly good."

The camera pulled back further to show the old woman standing beside the couch. With her was a group of figures from a nightmare. Some of them had horns. Some had prehensile tails. Others had hands instead of feet, or pebbly lizard skin. In the dim, uncertain lighting, they looked like something out of a Bosch painting.

"This is the truth," Simeon said. "This is the reality. We know you believe this place was some kind of hippie paradise, but that's what you've been *programmed* to believe. What Potter has done—what she's still doing—is *monstrous*."

"None of this means anything," I told him. "You're a simulation, this is a bunch of faked footage."

The footage ended and Simeon reappeared, a stern look on his face. "Duke," he said sadly. "Think about it. What's the point of me coming all this way just to spin you some bullshit?"

"It's in character for the Bureau."

"With respect, Duke, you have no idea what's in character for the Bureau." He looked thoughtful. "You know, we've done this fifty times in the past three hundred years or so. We always lose contact with our ships, but sometimes we lose contact sooner rather than later, so we think sometimes you just shoot first and ask questions later. But they've always managed to get some word out. I'm guessing the thing you did to wreck my comms is new."

It wasn't new at all; the Punch was at least two hundred years old. I looked around *One Potato*'s flight deck and wondered what I was going to do.

"We've picked up quite a lot of data, down the years," he went on. "Tell me, do you hear voices?"

"What?"

He glanced at a display. "Is Karl Ross there? Ernestine Bury? Conjugación Lang?" He was watching my face as he said the names. "Sure, I could have hacked your comms, but how could I know who you were talking to?"

I leaned forward, closer to the display, the headache really starting to thump behind my eyes. "This is all bullshit," I told him. "You're an AI."

"They're Potter's students," he went on. "They all died busting her out of house arrest or stealing the colony carrier. The Bury girl was a psychopath; she killed fourteen people to get Potter aboard that carrier. They're dead, Duke. You're *all* dead. John Wayne Faraday committed suicide shortly after he quit the Bureau; Potter probably thought it would be funny to base you on him. There are no ships in this system but me. The other pilots are subroutines. Voices in your head, little bits of expertise and personality that you've externalised. The rock in that picture I showed you is a relay, a telefactor robot so you can talk to me in real-time. It's the size of a basketball. And you have to hold on, Duke. You have to calm down."

"What . . . ?" I felt confused. Everyone was trying to talk at once, the other pilots a rising tide of chatter.

"What you're thinking of doing. Every encounter we've had, the dewline has self-destructed. Potter's superbrights have come up with some kind of sub-quantum disruption effect—the explosion's visible from thousands of light-years away. It takes out the entire system, Duke. Sun and all. You have to calm down. You have to stop. You don't owe Potter anything; she left you behind like a guard dog."

"I'm not thinking of doing anything," I told him, but the headache was getting worse, a great pressure growing against my temples. Suddenly, Simeon being an AI made perfect sense. Why send people into a system that was about to go bang?

"This has to stop, Duke," he was saying. "Millions of people have died already in the ships you've destroyed in other systems. You can help us. You can help make sure no one else dies. We need to find Potter and stop her, stop this madness, and you have to calm down and not do anything silly."

I had a sudden, disorienting sensation that I was huge, all-encompassing, looking down on the system like a woozy god. I could see *Gregor Samsa* and a tiny ball of rock floating nearby, and knew it was *One Potato, Two Potato*. Knew it was me.

"I *am* calm," I said, and *concentrated.*

———————

It was the morning after the morning after my hundred and fiftieth birthday, and a terrible noise was trying to wake me up.

About the Author

DAVE HUTCHINSON was born in Sheffield in 1960 and read American Studies at the University of Nottingham before becoming a journalist. He's the author of five collections of short stories and four novels. His novella *The Push* was nominated for the BSFA Award in 2010, and his novels *Europe in Autumn* and *Europe at Midnight* were nominated for the BSFA, Arthur C. Clarke, and John W. Campbell Memorial Awards in 2015 and 2016 respectively. *Europe at Midnight* was also short-listed for a Kitschie Award in 2016. He now writes full-time, and lives in North London.

Dave Hutchinson

TOR·COM

**Science fiction. Fantasy. The universe.
And related subjects.**

*

More than just a publisher's website, *Tor.com*
is a venue for **original fiction, comics,** and
discussion of the entire field of SF and fantasy,
in all media and from all sources. Visit our site
today—and join the conversation yourself.